STARS OF SPORT

TIGER WOODS

BY MICHAEL V. USCHAN

KIDHAVEN
PRESS™

THOMSON

GALE

San Diego • Detroit • New York • San Francisco • Cleveland
New Haven, Conn. • Waterville, Maine • London • Munich

To future champions (in life and sports) Karley,
Cameron, and Chloe Morotta.

LIBRARY OF CONGRESS CATALOGING-IN-PUBLICATION DATA

Uschan, Michael V., 1948–
  Tiger Woods / by Michael V. Uschan.
    p. cm.—(Stars of sport)
Summary: Discusses the early childhood abilities, golf championships, master golfer
status, and continued successes of Tiger Woods.
Includes bibliographical references (p.   ).
  ISBN 0-7377-1397-6 (hardback : alk. paper)
1. Woods, Tiger— Juvenile literature. 2. Golfers—United States—Biography—Juvenile
literature. [1. Woods, Tiger. 2. Golfers. 3. Racially mixed people—Biography.] I. Title.
II. Series.
  GV964 .W66 U73 2003
  796.352'092—dc21

                                                              2002004103

Printed in the United States of America

Contents

Born to Stardom

Golf is a game that began in Scotland more than six centuries ago. The greatest player this ancient sport has ever seen was born on December 30, 1975, in Cypress, California. His parents are Earl and Kultida Woods. They named him Eldrick Thon Woods. This great golfer says his parents gave him an unusual first name to show how much they loved him. "When I was growing up, my parents loved to remind me that I was named Eldrick for a special reason. The 'E' at the beginning represents Earl and the 'K' at the end stands for Kultida. My mother and father wanted their initials to encompass [wrap around] my name so that I would always be surrounded by my parents."[1]

Woods always knew his parents loved him. And that love gave him the supreme confidence he needed to achieve great things.

Eldrick received another special name from his father, a soldier in the U.S. Army who fought in the Vietnam War. During the war Earl had become friends with Vuong Dang Phong, a colonel in the South Vietnamese army

Tiger Woods smiles broadly after winning another championship. As a child, the love of his family gave him the confidence to achieve great things.

nicknamed "Tiger" because he was a fierce fighter. Earl began calling his infant son "Tiger" in honor of his friend, who was killed in the war. It was as "Tiger" that Eldrick would become known as the greatest golfer ever.

Watching Dad Play

Earl and Kultida met during the Vietnam War while Earl was serving in Thailand, her homeland. She came to America and they were married in 1973. When Earl retired from the army a year later, they moved to California.

Earl loved to play golf. He spent many hours hitting balls into a net in the family's garage. When Tiger was just a few months old he began watching his dad. When Tiger was seven months old Earl gave his son a cut-down putter as a toy. Tiger dragged it around the house wherever he went. Earl once bragged he introduced his son to golf at a very early age, "When most kids are in those circular walkers," Woods said, "you give them a rattle. He had a putter."[2]

One day when Tiger was ten months old, he was watching Earl hit balls. When his father took a break Tiger climbed out of his high chair, put a ball on the practice mat, and swung at it. He knocked it solidly into the net. Earl was amazed his son could hit the ball so well. He ran into the house, shouting to Kultida, "We have a genius on our hands."[3]

Child Prodigy

Tiger was a "child prodigy," the term for a boy or girl who shows amazing abilities at a very young age. The famous musician Mozart, for example, could compose songs

Tiger's father, Earl, studies Tiger's putting prowess during a practice round at Pebble Beach, California. Earl took Tiger golfing for the first time when Tiger was only two years old.

when he was five. Tiger's talent was that he was able to golf at an age when other boys and girls could not.

Tiger's natural balance and coordination had helped him strike the ball so well. But the infant was also able to perform this remarkable feat because his father began preparing him to golf from the time he was born. And Earl kept teaching Tiger how to hit the ball even though he was still just a baby.

His dad took Tiger to a golf course for the first time when he was two years old. The first hole Tiger played was 410 yards long. Tiger had to hit the ball eight times to get it on the **green** and needed three putts to sink it in the hole. Although his score of 11 was seven **strokes** over **par**, it was a remarkable achievement for someone that young. It was not long before Tiger was playing much better. A day before his fourth birthday Tiger had a score of

48 for nine holes, and by age six he could already hit the ball 126 yards and had twice made a **hole-in-one.**

When Tiger first started at four years old, he began taking lessons from Rudy Duran, a professional teacher at Heartwell Park Golf Course in nearby Long Beach. Duran helped Tiger learn to hit the ball better and taught him other things that helped him play better.

As Tiger was growing up, other people also helped him improve. They included golf teachers John Anselmo and Butch Harmon, and Jay Brunza, a psychologist who gave Tiger tips on how to concentrate better when he golfed.

The effort to make Tiger into a great golfer was a team effort and the people who helped him became

Sixteen-year-old Tiger tees off. In 1992, Tiger was the youngest player ever to compete in a PGA event.

(Left to right) Tiger's parents, Earl and Kultida Woods, and Elin Nordegren, his girlfriend, applaud as Tiger is awarded the Green Jacket as the 2002 Masters champion.

known as Team Tiger. It was also an expensive effort, and some years his parents had to pay as much as $25,000 for lessons, equipment, course fees, and travel to tournaments.

A Family Decision

It was easy for Tiger's parents to realize their son had a special gift. And even when Tiger was only a few years old, Earl and Kultida had already decided they should do everything they could to help him become the best player he could. "To our family," Earl admitted, "the big picture became Tiger's extraordinary ability, and how to nurture it."[4]

Training a Tiger

Tiger Woods would never have been able to become a great golfer without his parents. The sacrifices Earl and Kultida Woods made in time and money helped their son keep improving so that he would one day be good enough to challenge the world's greatest golfers.

Learning from Dad

Earl did not play golf until he was in his forties, but by the time Tiger was born he had worked hard to make himself a good player. He taught Tiger the fundamentals of this difficult sport—like how to hit the ball and **putt** it on the green. Earl even cut down some of his old clubs so his young son would have clubs he could easily swing.

Earl taught his son other important lessons. He wanted Tiger to be mentally tough when he competed against other golfers. He wanted him to believe he could win every time he played. Earl did this by constantly telling Tiger he was a good player. The praise helped Tiger become confident. He also told Tiger he must never give up, even when it looked like he might lose.

Earl looks on while Tiger sizes up an important putt at the 1998 AT&T National Pro-Am tournament.

When Tiger was seven years old, Earl began some unusual training. As Tiger was preparing to hit the ball or make a putt, Earl would make a loud noise. He imitated bird sounds, coughed, and dropped his clubs on the ground so they rattled noisily.

Earl was trying to help Tiger improve his concentration so that nothing would upset him while he was playing. It worked. One of Tiger's greatest strengths is that nothing bothers him when he is golfing.

Tiger hugs his dad after winning his first Masters in 1997 with a record-breaking score. Earl's training had prepared his son to be the best.

Tiger's mom, Kultida, embraces him as the third-time U.S. Amateur golf champion in 1996.

Lessons from Mom

Kultida did not play golf, but she also helped her son in many ways. She drove him to courses to practice and to tournaments where he competed. Kultida also taught her son many important lessons about life.

Tiger was a fierce competitor who always wanted to win. And Tiger almost always did win, even when he played much older golfers. Once after he lost to an adult,

Tiger's rich racial background includes Caucasian, Black, Indian (Native American), and Asian—a blend he, as a teenager, dubbed Cablinasian.

the six-year-old became angry and refused to shake hands with the winner. Kultida scolded Tiger for his conduct, saying, "You must be a sportsman, win or lose."[5]

Kultida also taught Tiger about racism. His mother is Asian. His father's family includes ancestors who were African American, Indian (Native American), and Caucasian. When Tiger was a teenager, he made up a name to describe his rich racial heritage. He called himself *Cablinasian*, which he said stood for Caucasian, Black, Indian, and Asian.

His mother had to explain racism to Tiger because he encountered it at an early age. On his first day in kindergarten in September 1981, some older white boys called him "monkey" and yelled other racial slurs. When Tiger played golf, he sometimes heard similar ugly remarks from people watching him. His mother told Tiger something that helped him deal with such ugly behavior by other people. "Racism," she said, "is not your problem, it's theirs. Just play your game."[6] It was something Tiger never forgot.

A Happy Childhood

Golf was the most important thing in Tiger's life while he was growing up. But it was not the only thing he cared about. Tiger liked school and was a good student—he graduated from Anaheim West High School with a 3.79 grade point average. Tiger also enjoyed running. In junior high school he competed in cross-country and track events like the 400-meter race.

Tiger says his early years were not much different from those of other children. "Hey," he once said, "I had a normal childhood. I did the same things every kid did. I studied and went to the mall. I was addicted to TV wrestling, rap music and 'The Simpsons.' I got into trouble and got out of it. I loved my parents and obeyed [them]."[7]

Although most young people Tiger knew were golfers, he had other friends. Tiger sometimes took a few days off from golf so he could spend time with these friends. They would play computer video games, ride their bikes, and do other things kids their age did. But Tiger never stayed away from golf too long—he loved it too much.

Tiger Becomes Famous

People become famous for two main reasons. They can be well known for their great skill and many accomplishments like Michael Jordan, who is considered the greatest basketball player ever. Or they can become known to millions of people because they have an unusual or unique quality, like being the world's oldest or tallest person.

Tiger Woods became famous for both reasons. And it started happening when he was a small child.

A Television Appearance

Tiger first became known to the public because of his amazing golf skills from the age of two. Like many proud mothers, Kultida liked to brag about her son. When she called a Los Angeles television station to tell it about her son's ability, a reporter did a news story about Tiger. When the story aired on television, thousands of people began to learn about this unusual young golfer.

The story brought Tiger to the attention of the *Mike Douglas Show*, a nationally televised daytime talk show, and Tiger was invited to be on the show. On October 6, 1978, Tiger came on stage wearing shorts, a red cap, and carrying his bag of cut-down clubs.

The audience applauded the smiling two-year-old. And they cheered Tiger even louder when he hit solid

Tiger and Earl pose for photographers after yet another of Tiger's amateur triumphs on his road to fame and fortune.

drives into a net and made some putts in a contest against Bob Hope, a famous comedian who also loved golf.

Millions of television watchers had seen Tiger. When he was five years old, *Golf Digest* magazine did a story on him because he played so well, and many more people learned about him. People across the country were beginning to know who Tiger was.

Winning Tournaments

Tiger first became famous because no one so young had ever played golf so well. As Tiger grew older he also started becoming known to millions of sports fans because he was winning important tournaments.

In 1984 when Tiger was eight years old, he won the Optimist International Junior World Championship for his age bracket, which included golfers eight to ten years old. He would win five more Junior World titles, more than anyone else ever had. In 1991 when he was fifteen, Tiger became the youngest player to win the U.S. Junior **Amateur** Championship. Tiger was often the youngest to win a tournament, and every victory made him more famous.

Tiger's fame grew again in 1992, but not because he won a tournament. Instead, at the age of only sixteen, Tiger qualified to play in the Los Angeles Open, an event for **professional** golfers. Tiger was the youngest person ever to play in a **Professional Golfers' Association (PGA) Tour** event.

Tiger had made golf history in the Los Angeles Open. But he was not satisfied because he had not played very

Tiger directs a long putt during the opening round of the 1992 Los Angeles Open, his first PGA event.

well, at least in comparison with the other golfers. He did not want just to play with the pros—he wanted to beat them. But even Tiger knew he had to improve before that could happen. "I'm not mature enough," Tiger told reporters, who were amazed he had even qualified for such an event. "My body hasn't finished growing and my swing's not good enough."[8]

Although Tiger had reached his full height of six feet, two inches, he was skinny, weighing only 140 pounds.

He knew he had to gain weight, grow stronger, and become a better golfer before he could beat the pros.

Amateur Champion

Tiger, however, was good enough to beat players his own age. When Tiger was a freshman at Anaheim Western High School, he won twenty-seven of twenty-nine tournaments. In 1993 when he was a senior, Tiger received the Dial Award as the nation's best high school player. Tiger also made golf history in high school by becoming the first golfer to win the U.S. Junior Amateur tournament three straight years.

When Tiger graduated he began attending Stanford University on a golf scholarship. Although Tiger won many college tournaments including the 1996 National Collegiate Athletic Association individual title, his biggest victories were not in college competition. It was in the more important Men's U.S. Amateur Championship where Tiger really made his mark on amateur golf.

The Men's U.S. Amateur Championship is a very hard tournament. After two rounds of **stroke play**, the sixty-four golfers with the lowest scores advance to match play to determine the champion. In match play, two golfers are paired for eighteen holes. Golfers try to capture individual holes by recording the lowest score on each hole, and the winner is the one who wins the most holes.

Tiger won his first amateur title in August 1994, just a few weeks before he began attending Stanford. He defeated Trip Kuehne, a twenty-two-year-old Oklahoma State junior, in a dramatic come-from-behind victory in which he won five of the last nine holes. At the age of seventeen, Tiger was the youngest U.S. Men's Amateur champion ever. He was also the first African American golfer to win this important tournament.

Tiger cheers after sinking the winning putt in the 1993 Honda Classic. He would be the amateur champion before he even entered college.

Tiger poses with the trophy awarded him for winning the 1994 U.S. Amateur Championship.

An African American Hero

Tiger's early fame was based mainly on the fact that his skill was so amazing for someone so young. But as Tiger grew older and began winning important tournaments, people began to know about him for another reason. And that was his race.

The sport had been dominated by whites ever since golfers began hitting balls in Scotland. This was true even in America, where people had played since the late 1800s.

African Americans had never had many opportunities to play because of discrimination. For much of the twentieth century African Americans were not allowed on many golf courses, even public courses run by local governments. They were also barred from competing in major amateur and professional tournaments.

This injustice began to end in the 1960s when African Americans started winning their long battle against discrimination. As a result, more minority golfers began playing. But until Tiger came along, no African American had ever been considered a great golfer.

Like most African Americans his age, Tiger's father never had a chance to play when he was growing up. That was one reason why he had been so determined Tiger would have every opportunity to become a great golfer. "See, this is the first intuitive black golfer ever raised in the United States," he said. "He knew how to swing a golf club before he could walk."[9]

As he got older, Tiger was showing the entire world that an African American could play as well as any white golfer. This made him even more famous.

Becoming a Master Golfer

I n April 1995 Tiger Woods played in the Masters Tournament for the first time. Although the Masters is one of the four major professional golf tournaments, he was invited to play because he had won the 1994 Men's U.S. Amateur Championship.

Tiger has always respected the history of the game he plays so well. And Augusta National, the Georgia course where the Masters is held each year, is one of the world's most historic courses. One of the people who designed the course in the 1930s was Bobby Jones, one of the greatest players in golf's history. The golfers who had won the Masters included the best ever to play the game.

The eighteen-year-old amateur showed he belonged in the field with the world's finest golfers. He finished

Fans and competitors alike watch with fascination as Tiger makes a long drive off the tee at the 1995 Masters tournament.

forty first with a score of 293, just fifteen shots behind winner Ben Crenshaw.

While talking to reporters after the third round, Tiger pointed to photographs of past champions and made a prediction. "Someday," he said with a smile, "I'm going to get my picture up there."[10] It would happen sooner than anyone thought possible.

Tiger tees off in the final match of the 1995 U.S. Amateur championship in Newport, Rhode Island.

Turning Pro

On August 25, 1996, Tiger won his third straight Men's U.S. Amateur title. He had already made golf history as the first African American amateur champion. Now Tiger was the first to win it three straight years, an incredible achievement.

But Tiger was bored with playing against, and beating, amateurs. He wanted to challenge the world's best players. So on August 28 Tiger made an announcement that changed his life: "I guess, hello, world."[11] That was how Tiger opened a news conference to announce he was becoming a professional golfer. The next day Tiger made his professional debut in the first round of the Greater Milwaukee Open.

Tiger was not only saying "hello" to the world of pro golf but to a world filled with riches and even more fame. The phrase he opened his news conference with appeared in television ads for Nike, one of several firms that signed him to endorsement contracts worth more than $60 million. He was not only a pro, but a rich one.

Surprising the World

Most golf writers predicted Tiger would struggle against professionals. His first challenge came in August 1996, when he tied for sixtieth place in the Greater Milwaukee Open. It was a less than stellar debut for someone accustomed to winning.

But Tiger soon proved the so-called experts wrong. On October 6, 1996, Tiger won his first pro tournament, the Las Vegas Invitational. People were stunned that he had been able to win a pro event so quickly. He followed that up with another victory two weeks later at the Walt Disney World Classic. That tournament was in Orlando, Florida, where he had already bought a home with his new wealth.

His debut was so sensational that *Golf Digest* magazine a few months later ran a story with a bold headline that asked, "Is this Kid Superman?" Tiger, however, had always known he would become a great player. As he said after winning in Las Vegas, "I don't see any of this as scary or a burden. I've always known where I wanted to go in life. This is my purpose [winning tournaments to become known as a great golfer]."[12]

Tiger was so successful in the final months of the 1996 season that people wondered if his brilliant play had been a fluke. But the young star showed he was for real in January 1997 by winning the Mercedes Championship, an event limited to golfers who had won tournaments the previous year. In the first tournament of the season Tiger had beaten the best golfers in the world. In February he also captured the Asian Honda Classic in Thailand. He shared the victory with his mother, who joyously returned to her homeland with her famous son.

Tiger poses with his trophy, after winning his first pro tournament, the Las Vegas Invitational, in October 1996.

Tiger and his mom smile for the cameras after Tiger won the Asian Honda Classic in 1997 in Bangkok, Thailand, his mother's homeland.

His brilliant play made Tiger one of the favorites heading into the Masters that April. When Tiger got off to a disastrous start by shooting 4-over-par 40 for the first nine holes, it looked like he had no chance to win. But something amazing happened. Tiger made a correction in his swing, shortening it so he could hit the ball straighter, and began playing like the superstar everyone thought he was. His score for the second nine holes was 6-under-par 30, which gave him a 2-under-par 70 total.

Tiger waits with anticipation for his putt to drop into the cup for the win at the 1997 Masters.

After one round Tiger trailed leader John Huston by three shots. But in the next two days Tiger shot wonderfully low scores of 66 and 65 and had an incredible nine-shot lead after the first three rounds. Tiger always wears a red shirt for good luck on the final day of a tournament if he is confident he will win. Whether his lucky charm helped or not is debatable. But in the final round on

Sunday (April 13) Tiger was brilliant. He shot a 3-under-par 69 to win his first major tournament.

Tiger made history that day in one of the oldest, most important of all golf tournaments. At the age of twenty-one years, three months, and fourteen days, Tiger was the youngest player to win a Masters. More significantly, Tiger was the first African American to win the Masters or any other **major.**

After Tiger made his final putt he went to his father who was standing nearby. He hugged him, saying, "We did it, Pop! We did it!"[13] The baby boy who had begun hitting golf balls in a garage with his dad so many years before was now the Masters champion!

African American Victory

Another person Tiger hugged that day was black golfer Charlie Sifford. Tiger knew that if Sifford and other African American golfers had not won their battle to play professional golf, he would never have been able to play in the Masters.

Tiger also realized that winning at Augusta National was special. The course was in the Deep South, where racism had always been strongest. Cliff Roberts, one of Augusta's founders, had once claimed, "As long as I'm alive, golfers [at Augusta] will be white, and **caddies** will be black."[14]

Even though Roberts was dead by the time Tiger won, his victory was a wonderful symbol of how golf had been able to escape its racist past.

CHAPTER FIVE

Is Tiger the Greatest Golfer Ever?

His record-setting Masters victory was so over-powering and dominating that some people be-gan to believe that Tiger Woods might be the greatest golfer ever born. He was already the finest African American who had ever played. But that was far from enough for Tiger. After winning his first Men's U.S. Am-ateur championship he had boldly proclaimed, "I don't want to be the greatest minority golfer ever. I want to be the greatest golfer ever."[15]

Tiger's idol while he was growing up was Jack Nick-laus, who at the time was considered the finest player ever. One reason Nicklaus is considered the best is that he has won more major tournaments than anyone else—eighteen of them. Tiger knew he would have to win more majors than Nicklaus had before people would consider him the greater golfer.

But even after winning the Masters, Tiger knew how hard it would be to surpass his former idol. So after his historic victory Tiger did a strange thing. He and Butch Harmon, his golf coach, decided to refine his swing so that he would never struggle again like he did in the first nine holes of the Masters. It seemed hard to believe that Tiger could get any better. But the changes he would make would lead to even greater accomplishments.

Tiger receives the College Player of the Year award from Jack Nicklaus, his childhood idol.

Golf Can Be Hard

Winning had come easily to Tiger in his first few months as a professional. But after his historic Masters victory Tiger failed to win another tournament the rest of the season. "Golf humbles you every day, every shot, really. I know how hard the game is," he could now say.[16]

Sportswriters began proclaiming that Tiger was in a slump. However, the reason he lost was that he was changing his swing. With Harmon's help Tiger was developing a more compact stroke which would make him a more consistent player. But it took Tiger a long time to learn to play well with his new swing, and in 1998 he won only one tournament and played poorly in the majors.

Tiger, however, came roaring back in 1999, capturing eight tournaments and once again establishing himself as the world's greatest golfer. One of his wins was in the PGA Championship, giving him his second major title. But this brilliant season was only a prelude to the greatest year any golfer ever had.

The Tiger Slam

In 2000 Tiger dominated golf by winning nine tournaments including the year's final three majors—the U.S. Open, British Open, and PGA Championship. With his victory at the British Open, Tiger had won all the majors at least once for what is called a "Career Grand Slam." At age twenty-four, he was the youngest player to have won all four majors. It was fitting that his history-making feat occurred on St. Andrews, the course in

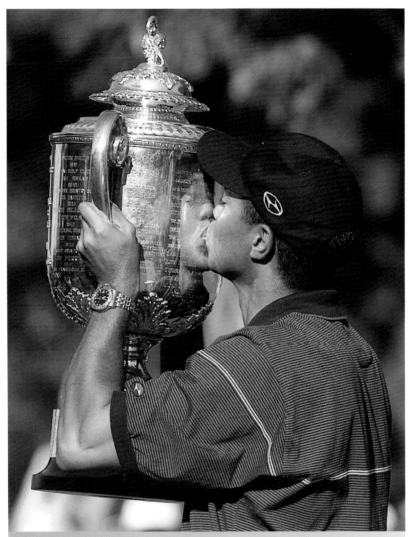

Tiger kisses the trophy he won for the 1999 PGA Championship. It was the second major tournament victory of his career.

Scotland considered the birthplace of golf. The sport has been played there for over six centuries.

Tiger was only the second golfer to win three majors in one season—the first was Ben Hogan in 1953. And Tiger had dominated those three majors like no other golfer ever had, setting records for winning margins in all three. His incredible fifteen-shot victory in the U.S. Open at Pebble Beach was also the largest victory margin in any major tournament ever played. Tiger thus surpassed even "Old" Tom Morris, a legendary Scottish golfer who previously held the record for any major after winning the 1862 British Open by thirteen strokes.

In April 2001 Tiger made golf history again when he won the Masters for his fourth consecutive major, making him the first golfer to hold all four major titles at the same time. His victory ignited a controversy over whether Tiger had achieved a "Grand Slam." The term "Grand Slam" was first used in 1930 when Bobby Jones shocked the golf world by winning the Men's U.S. Amateur, U.S. Open, British Amateur, and British Open titles. Today the term "Grand Slam" means winning all four major professional tournaments in one year, something no one has ever done.

Tiger, however, had not won all four titles in the same calendar year. Although everyone realized it was an historic accomplishment, a debate raged over whether it was a true "Grand Slam." Eventually, sportswriters came up with a new term that was perfect. They called it the "Tiger Slam," an amazing feat by perhaps the most amazing player in the game's long history.

Is Tiger the Greatest?

By the time Tiger turned twenty-six on December 30, 2001, he had firmly established himself as one of the greatest golfers who has ever played. In less than five full

Tiger and Kultida Woods pose for a photograph after he won the 2001 U.S. Open.

Important Dates in the Life of Tiger Woods

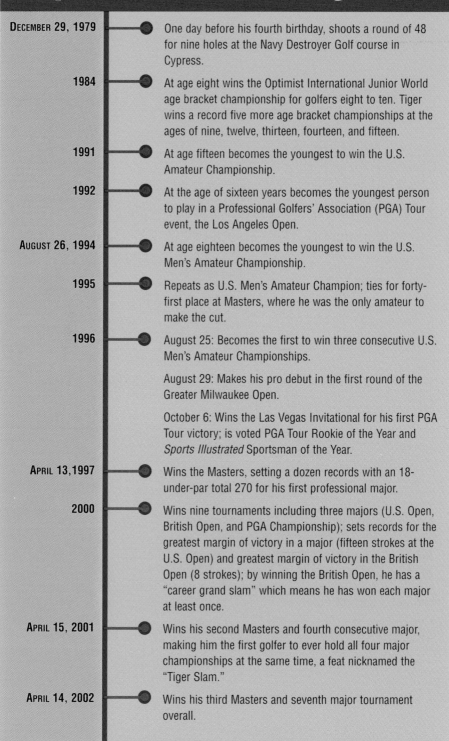

DECEMBER 29, 1979 — One day before his fourth birthday, shoots a round of 48 for nine holes at the Navy Destroyer Golf course in Cypress.

1984 — At age eight wins the Optimist International Junior World age bracket championship for golfers eight to ten. Tiger wins a record five more age bracket championships at the ages of nine, twelve, thirteen, fourteen, and fifteen.

1991 — At age fifteen becomes the youngest to win the U.S. Amateur Championship.

1992 — At the age of sixteen years becomes the youngest person to play in a Professional Golfers' Association (PGA) Tour event, the Los Angeles Open.

AUGUST 26, 1994 — At age eighteen becomes the youngest to win the U.S. Men's Amateur Championship.

1995 — Repeats as U.S. Men's Amateur Champion; ties for forty-first place at Masters, where he was the only amateur to make the cut.

1996 — August 25: Becomes the first to win three consecutive U.S. Men's Amateur Championships.

August 29: Makes his pro debut in the first round of the Greater Milwaukee Open.

October 6: Wins the Las Vegas Invitational for his first PGA Tour victory; is voted PGA Tour Rookie of the Year and *Sports Illustrated* Sportsman of the Year.

APRIL 13,1997 — Wins the Masters, setting a dozen records with an 18-under-par total 270 for his first professional major.

2000 — Wins nine tournaments including three majors (U.S. Open, British Open, and PGA Championship); sets records for the greatest margin of victory in a major (fifteen strokes at the U.S. Open) and greatest margin of victory in the British Open (8 strokes); by winning the British Open, he has a "career grand slam" which means he has won each major at least once.

APRIL 15, 2001 — Wins his second Masters and fourth consecutive major, making him the first golfer to ever hold all four major championships at the same time, a feat nicknamed the "Tiger Slam."

APRIL 14, 2002 — Wins his third Masters and seventh major tournament overall.

seasons Tiger had won twenty-nine pro tournaments in the United States and six more overseas in countries like Germany, Japan, and Thailand. And six of his victories had been in major tournaments—a third of the record total eighteen championships it took Nicklaus three decades to accumulate.

Tiger added two more titles to his majors record in 2002, raising the total to eight. He won his third Masters title in April 2002 and his second U.S. Open championship in May. At this point he is clearly on pace to surpass the accomplishments of Nicklaus, who won his first of eighteen majors (the U.S. Open) in 1962 and his last (the Masters) in 1986 when he was forty-four. Although many people believe Tiger has already earned the right to be considered the greatest golfer ever after his "Tiger Slam," some believe it is too early to make that judgement. Among the latter is the legendary Sam Snead, who won a record eighty-one pro tournaments in a long career from 1937 to 1979.

Snead admits to being awed by the young golfer's skills. But Snead warns against being too hasty to assess Tiger's place in golf history. "Let time go on a little bit first," advises the golfing legend. "Give him a little while longer. What's the rush? He's the best right now, that's for sure, but he's [still young] and he's got a long way to go."[17]

Snead is right. With several more decades left to play competitive golf, there is no hurry to figure out where Tiger ranks in the history of golf. His legacy most likely will be as the greatest golfer ever to have played the game. But only time will tell.

Notes

Chapter One: Born to Stardom

1. Quoted in Earl Woods with Pete McDaniel, *Training a Tiger: A Father's Guide to Raising a Winner in Both Golf and Life.* New York: HarperCollins, 1997, p. 3.
2. Quoted in Tim Rosaforte, *Tiger Woods, The Makings of a Champion.* New York: St. Martin's Press, 1997, p. 17.
3. Quoted in John Strege, *Tiger: A Biography of Tiger Woods.* New York: Broadway Books, 1997, p. 11.
4. Quoted in Woods with McDaniel, *Training A Tiger,* p. 99.

Chapter Two: Training a Tiger

5. Quoted in Strege, *Tiger,* p. 21.
6. Quoted in Jeff Savage, *Tiger Woods: King of the Course.* Minneapolis: Lerner Publications, 1998, p. 33.
7. Quoted in Curry Kirkpatrick, "A Tiger in the Grass," *Newsweek,* April 10, 1995, p. 72.

Chapter Three: Tiger Becomes Famous

8. Quoted in Rosaforte, *Tiger Woods,* p. 69.

9. Quoted in Rick Reilly, "Goodness Gracious, He's a Great Ball of Fire," *Sports Illustrated*, March 27, 1995. p. 66.

Chapter Four: Becoming a Master Golfer

10. John Garrity, *Tiger Woods: The Making of a Champion*. New York: Simon & Schuster, 1997, p. 44.
11. Quoted in Gary D'Amato, "It's official: Woods Era Dawns," *Milwaukee Journal-Sentinel*, August 29, 1996, p. C1.
12. Quoted in Gary Smith, "The Chosen One," *Sports Illustrated*, December 23, 1996, p. 32.
13. Quoted in Earl Woods with Fred Mitchell, *Playing Through, Straight Talk on Hard Work, Big Dreams and Adventures with Tiger*. New York: HarperCollins, 1998, p. 165.
14. Quoted in Rick Reilly, "Strokes of Genius," *Sports Illustrated*, April 21, 1997, p. 30.
15. Quoted in "Tiger Timeline," *CNN/Sports Illustrated*. www.sportsillustrated.cnn.com.
16. Quoted in Jaime Diaz, "Masters Plan," *Sports Illustrated*. April 13, 1998, p. 65.
17. Quoted in Thomas Bonk. "Is Tiger Woods the Greatest Golfer?" *Los Angeles Times*, June 20, 2000.

Glossary

amateur: Someone who plays golf for the love of the sport.

caddie: Someone who carries a golfer's clubs.

drive (or tee-shot): The golfer's first shot on each hole.

eagle: A score on a hole that is two strokes under par.

green: Extremely short-cut grass on which the player putts to get the ball in the hole.

hole-in-one (or ace): A tee-shot that lands in the hole.

major: One of four major championships in men's professional golf: the British Open, the Masters, the Professional Golfers' Association Championship, and the United States Open.

par: The score a good player should make on a particular hole—3, 4, or 5 depending on its rating—or the total number of strokes required to play the entire course.

professional: Someone who plays golf to make money.

Professional Golfers' Association Tour: The organization that runs professional golf tournaments.

putt: One stroke taken on the green.

stroke: Counted in the score every time a player strikes the ball.

stroke play (or medal play): A tournament decided by the number of strokes players take.

For Further Exploration

Books

William Durbin, *Tiger Woods*. New York: Chelsea House, 1998.

Nicholas Edwards, *Tiger Woods: A Driving Master*. New York: Scholastic, 1997.

Bill Gutman, *Tiger Woods: A Biography*. New York: Peoples Books, 1997.

S.A. Kramer, *Tiger Woods: Golfing to Greatness*. New York: Random House, 1997.

Richard Rambeck, *Tiger Woods*. New York: Child's World, 1998.

Jeff Savage, *Tiger Woods: King of the Course*. Minneapolis: Lerner Publications, 1998.

Mark Stewart, *Tiger Woods: Driving Force*. New York: Childrens Press, 1998.

Earl Woods with Pete McDaniel, *Training A Tiger: A Father's Guide to Raising a Winner in Both Golf and Life*. New York: HarperCollins, 1997.

Videos

Tiger Woods: Son, Hero & Champion, Trans World International, CBS Video, 1997.

The Tiger Woods Story, Paramount Home Video, 1998.

Website

Tiger Woods (www.tigerwoods.com). His official website includes information, pictures, videos, and other interesting features.

Index

Picture Credits

Cover photo: © Temp Sports/CORBIS

© AFP/CORBIS, 35

Associated Press, AP, 5, 7, 8, 12, 13, 19, 29, 33

David Cannon/Allsport, 25

J.D. Cuban/Allsport, 26, 28

© Duomo/CORBIS, 17, 21

Rusty Jarrett/Allsport, 22

Steve Munday/Allsport, 30

Brandy Noon, 38

© Reuters NewMedia, Inc./CORBIS, 9

Jamie Squire/Allsport, 11, 37

Yearbookarchive.com, 14

About the Author

Michael V. Uschan has written more than twenty books, including biographies of baseball greats Hank Aaron and Mark McGwire and Olympic heroes Jim Thorpe, Jesse Owens, and Eric Heiden. He is the recipient of the Council for Wisconsin Writers 2001 Juvenile Nonfiction award for his book, *The Korean War*. Uschan began his career as a writer and editor with United Press International, a wire service that provides stories to newspapers, radio, and television. Journalism is sometimes called "history in a hurry." Uschan considers writing history books a natural extension of skills he developed in his many years as a working journalist. He and his wife, Barbara, reside in the Milwaukee suburb of Franklin, Wisconsin.